Robert Loveman

Poems

Robert Loveman

Poems

ISBN/EAN: 9783337156466

Printed in Europe, USA, Canada, Australia, Japan

Cover: Foto ©Andreas Hilbeck / pixelio.de

More available books at **www.hansebooks.com**

Poems

By

Robert Loveman

Philadelphia

J. B. Lippincott Company

Mdcccxcvii

Table of Contents

6

TO

MY SISTERS LINKA AND ANNE

MY JOSEPHINE

THERE was a France, there was a queen,
There was another Josephine,
Whose gentle love and tender art
Subdued Napoleon's soldier heart.

But she of France was ne'er, I ween,
Fairer than thou, my Josephine;
To storm thy heart I'll boldly plan,
God! if I were the Corsican!

OCTOBER

In April mortal's eye hath seen
The waking woods arrayed in green,
While every birdling of the throng
Essayed sweet syllables of song.

And now October wooes the wold
To dreams of crimson and of gold;
The laughing leaves, all out of breath,
Are dancing down to dusty death.

DREAMS

DREAMS, like children hand in hand,
Wander through the shadow-land ;
All the night they softly creep
Down the corridors of sleep.

Dreams, like children, laugh and weep
In the mystic house of sleep ;
Then hand in hand they run away,
Frightened by the noisy day.

YON STAR

Yon star that glitters in the east
Shone o'er Belshazzar's fated feast,
Or lighted up the evening sky
For Esther and for Mordecai.

Yon star looked down with sleepless lids
Upon the rising pyramids,
And shall illume the final gust
That levels them to desert dust.

IN VENICE

In Venice, on the Rialto,
A merry mass of people go ;
The siren city, like a bride,
Clings to the Adriatic's side ;
By day, by night, one still may hear
The soft song of the gondolier,
Whose oar is strong for friend or foe,
In Venice, on the Rialto.

In Venice, on the Rialto,
Homesick and lone, I weep with woe ;
Homesick and lone, what is to me
This marble city by the sea ?
One vision all my bosom fills—
O village in the Georgia hills,
For thee my heart is bended low,
In Venice, on the Rialto !

NORTHPORT TOWN

In Northport town the sun goes down
Behind the hill, then all is still
Within the peaceful village, where
A benison is in the air.
A pilgrim host of crickets yield
An Angelus from every field;
And there the moon looks kindly down
In mellow beams on Northport town.

In Northport town—her eyes are brown,
Her hair as soft as any down
On any dove whose liquid note
Of love is heard within the cote.
Ah, this thy secret, village fair!
Ah, this thy charm, O village rare!
Heaven, rain thy sweetest odors down,
For Lottie lives in Northport town.

IN NAISHÁPÚR

In Naishápúr, when Omar wrote,
No nightingale with lusty throat
Carolled a clearer, sweeter note
    In Naishápúr.

He saw the yellow roses swoon
Beneath the kisses of the June,
And the star blossoms of the night
Opened their petals to his sight.

He sang of life, and death, and woe
A thousand years or so ago ;
The north winds o'er him rose-leaves throw
    In Naishápúr.

UPON A CRUTCH

Upon a crutch, her girlish face
Alight with love and tender grace,
Laughing, she limps from place to place
Upon a crutch.

And you and I, who journey through
A rose-leaf world of dawn and dew,
We cry to heaven overmuch,

We rail and frown at fate, while she,
And many more in agony,
Are brave and gentle, strong and true,
Upon a crutch.

A "LA FRANCE" ROSE

Thou art the rarest regal rose
The Summer in her glory shows,
With golden honey on thy lips,
Patrician to thy petals' tips.

If thou hadst bloomed in Paris, when
The Commune thronged with frenzied men,
Some Robespierre plant by weeds begat
Had slain thee, sweet aristocrat.

FROM FOREIGN LANDS

FROM foreign lands the ships come in
And greet the city's cheerful din,
Laden with love or steeped in sin,
    From foreign lands.

Yonder a giant cruiser bides
And struggles with the surging tides;
While, ill from grief and penury,

Through all the long night's mystery
A lonely man looks out to sea
And weeps for home and Italy,
    From foreign lands.

CLEOPATRA

EGYPT and Pharaoh and the Nile,
　A torrid vast of desert land,
Huge pyramids that grimly smile
　Across the shifting sand.

Egypt and Pharaoh, ay; but this—
　This Cleopatra wonders me,
Who leaped with many a burning kiss
　Into the arms of Antony.

THE VIGIL

Lest some sweet thought all unaware
Slip by me on the viewless air,
Lest some dear dream that softly stole
Past many a mighty poet-soul,

I'll in the morning sunshine sit,
And watch, and wait, and pray for it ;
Naught else possess my mind or eye,
Lest some sweet thought slip shyly by.

O ISRAEL!

O ISRAEL! thy glory gleamed
    Through ages long ago;
O Israel! a David dreamed
    Within thy tents of snow;
Thy warriors wise, and brave, and good,
Thy women queens of womanhood,
A pillared cloud, and manna food,
        O Israel! sweet Israel!

O Israel! again I see
    Thy chariot in the sky!
The seed of Abraham shall be
    Through all eternity;
Our fathers' faith, our fathers' God,
The paths of peace wherein they trod,
With love, with truth, thy soul be shod,
        O Israel! sweet Israel!

FROM FAR JAPAN

From far Japan a pretty fan
Hath come my lady's joy to plan,
With rapture her sweet face to scan,
From far Japan.

To touch the velvet of her hand
It journeyed over sea and land;
To flutter 'neath her lustrous eyes
Forsook the glow of Orient skies.

And yet I know it must be so,
The fan is happy.   I would go,
For her, forever to and fro
From far Japan.

TO-DAY'S RESOLVE

To-DAY no coward thought shall start
Upon its journey from my heart,
To-day no hasty word shall slip
Over the threshold of my lip.

To-day no selfish hope shall rest
Within the region of my breast,
To-day no wave of wrath shall roll
Over the ocean of my soul.

To-day I vow with sword and song
To fight oppression and the wrong,
To-day I dedicate my youth
To duty and eternal truth.

THE PARALYTIC

I.

He reads of the deeds of mighty men,
Of men in the brunt of battle, when,
With livid lips and bated breath
And loud huzzas, they dash to death.

II.

He reads of the deeds; his shrunken hands
Are tightly clinched; he understands
And feels, or why the storm
That rages through his helpless form?

THE WIND

I.

THE wind came up from the balmy south,
 Came merrily dancing everywhere;
He kissed my lady's rose-bud mouth
 And slept in the coils of her shining hair.

II.

Then waked and away to the sobbing sea,
 Swifter than hungry hawk or fox,
And angrily dashed, with demoniac glee,
 A giant ship against the rocks.

PURITY

Whose mind is pure, he is the man
For whom Almighty God doth plan;
For him in ecstasy the day
Doth blush itself in bliss away.

Whose heart is pure, for him the night
Visions and dreams of rare delight;
For him, beyond the sunset bars,
God sows the meadow sky with stars.

Whose soul is pure, for him the sea,
The mountain and its mystery;
For him, in all her shy retreats,
The tender heart of Nature beats.

Whose inmost thought, whose life is pure,
His soul is destined to endure,
To feel, to frame, to pray, to sing
In gardens of God's blossoming.

O MOTHER MINE!

O MOTHER mine! in other days,
Or ere I knew of blame or praise,
Thine was the love to light my ways,
      O mother mine!

And now, when Time, with tender touch,
Hath led thee gently down the years,
O mother mine! with tears, with tears,

I pray my care of thee be such
To pay in feeble part the debt,
If I have caused thee one regret,
      O mother mine!

OVER THE WAY

I.

OVER the way, on a bending bough,
A joyous bird is singing now,
Into the heart of the summer day
Trilling a merry roundelay.

II.

And over the way the blinds are drawn,
A mother's hope and love is gone;
Without, the song,—within, the gloom;
A babe lies dead in the darkened room.

NIAGARA

I.

SOME vast despair, some grief divine,
    Doth vigil keep
Forever here; before this shrine
    The waters weep.

II.

Methinks a God from some far sphere,
    In sportive part,
In ages past wooed Nature here,
    And broke her heart.

THE TRUANT

I.

In the last twilight dim and gray
From my fond clasp she slipped away,
As sweet a thought as ever stole
Into and out a poet's soul.

II.

And now, through all the weary night,
Within my heart I burn a light,
So my dear thought may enter when
She cometh weeping home again.

HER MAJESTY

I.

THE kingly Sun hath westward sped ;
    Now cometh soon,
By planet princes heralded,
    The maiden Moon.

II.

And as unto the throne of night
    She draweth near,
Each courtier star, with paling light,
    Doth disappear.

TROUBLE TOWN

As I came down from Trouble Town
I met an angel on the way,
A radiant angel on the way;
She looked into my aching eyes,—
O angel good and true and wise!—
She whispered hope,—O vision rare!—
She bade me bravely burdens bear,
She kissed away each fading frown
As I came down from Trouble Town.

I'm glad I've been to Trouble Town,
Else might I ne'er have known or seen.
Oh, hast thou never known or seen,
When struggling back to life and hope,
The vision on some sunny slope,
With eager arms and eyes of light,
While once again the earth was bright?
God, it is good that, king or clown,
We all must go to Trouble Town.

TO LONDON TOWN

To London town Will Shakespeare went,
Ambitious, eager, and intent,
To one vast end his being bent,
                    To London town.

He hugged his precious manuscript
Close to his heart, his fancy tripped
All feather-footed through the day.

And she—poor, lone Ann Hathaway—
Taught Judith, Hamnet, how to pray
For him—her lord, away, away
                    To London town.

SWEET ARE THE NAMES

SWEET are the names and Shakespeare's women, they
Like music melt upon the heart and ear;
First Juliet comes, then Beatrice draws near,
Perdita pure, and Lucrece chaste as day,
Dear Desdemona, she who loved the Moor,
There, poor Ophelia, and Cordelia here,
Whose voice was ever soft and low to Lear;
Rare Rosalind, the fair who reignèd o'er
Orlando's soul in Arden, Portia wise,
And Jessica, who with an unthrift love
Ran far as Belmont; look your last now, eyes,
On maid Miranda, gentle as a dove.
These names and women out of Shakespeare's art,
Like sweetest music, sway the human heart.

A SUNRISE

Up from the under wonder-world,
   A thousand battles won,
The east hath every flag unfurled:
   Good-morning, Signor Sun!

A SUNSET

A crimson, gray, and gold
   Enchantment to the eye;
Some artist saint spilled all his paint
   Adown the western sky.

POOR LITTLE ROSE

I know you, rose; I see you there,
Bathed in the balmy April air;
I've watched the weary winter through,
And seen the sun smile down on you,
Seen day by day your leaves grow green,
And baby buds spring up between;
So now small wonder that I feel
Thy charm, my mellow Maréchal Niel.
I know you, rose; your heart is won
By your fond love, the summer sun;
You sigh for him the long night through,
At morn your cheek is wet with dew,
With tears of dew, sweet loyal rose,
For oh, the night so slowly goes!

But when your lover sails the sky,
Ah, then again your cheek is dry,
And so I know your soul is won
By your fond love, the summer sun;
And yet, poor rose, ere many days,
Beneath his ardent burning rays,
E'en while he lightens earth and sky,
Thou then, sad queen, must drooping die,
And then he'll amorous glances throw
Upon some jaunty Jacqueminot,
And her torn heart will also feel
All thou hast known, my Maréchal Niel—
All of thy joys, all of thy woes,
Poor little rose,—poor little rose.

THE FREEBOOTER

DRUNKEN with dew, a bandit bee
    Across my flower-garden goes;
The noisy knave, what recketh he
    To stab a beetle, rob a rose?

IN AUTUMN

THE shepherd winds are driving
    Along the ways on high
A merry flock of cloudland sheep
    To meadows in the sky.

VERLAINE, VILLON, BAUDELAIRE

Verlaine, Villon, Baudelaire,
Delicacy and despair,
Perfume, poison, myrrh, and rue,
Bitter-sweet and honey-dew,
Lurid skies and absinthe air,
Verlaine, Villon, Baudelaire.

Verlaine, Villon, Baudelaire,
Chansonnette and rondeau rare,
Ballade, quatrain, villanelle,
Lovingly they wrought and well;
A fig for grief and carking care,
Verlaine, Villon, Baudelaire.

Verlaine, Villon, Baudelaire,—
The pity of it,—everywhere
About the world that men should be
Steeped to the eyes in poverty,
Then die like moths in glory's glare,
Verlaine, Villon, Baudelaire.

POETRY

O ART of arts! O gift of gifts!
    Sublimest of sublime!
To string the beaded thoughts into
    A rosary of rhyme.

WHERE DREAM-BOATS DRIFT

OVER the silver sea of sleep
    The dream-boats drift away, away,
Adown the dawn they softly creep
    Into the harbor of the day.

WORDS

WORDS, words, words
That bubble up from baby lips,
Or falter trembling forth when age
Upon the homeward journey slips
And stumbles ; words that rise
In prayer like incense to the skies,
Words that light with love the page,
Words, words, words.

Words, words, words
That poets borrow from the birds,
Willing words that have been caught
To the bosom of a thought;
Words of honey, words of gall,
Words that hold the heart in thrall,
Words sublime that chime and rhyme,
Words, words, words.

THE ANGELUS

THIS scene I see, this thought I feel,
　　Ah, distant days are glowing there,
When Millet's mother bade him kneel
　　And lisp in love his evening prayer.

THE MUSE

No sooner doth one song depart,
　　In fancy's realm to soar,
Another stands outside my heart
　　And taps upon the door.

ROSE IS THE GIRL

Rose is the girl; she bids me write
A rhyme for her, and I am quite
At loss for language adequate.
   Rose is the girl.

She is my life, my love, my fate,
To her my dreams are dedicate,
And when the moon shall shine to-night

I'll hie me to my lady's bower
And swear allegiance by the hour.
O Venus, Cupid, give me power!
   Rose is the girl.

A DREAMER

He is a dreamer, let him pass,
He reads the writing in the grass;
His seeing soul in rapture goes
Beyond the beauty of the rose.
He is a dreamer, and doth know
To sound the farthest depth of woe;
His days are calm, majestic, free;
He is a dreamer, let him be.

He is a dreamer; all the day
Blest visions throng him on his way,
Past the far sunset and the light,
Beyond the darkness and the night.
He is a dreamer—God! to be
Apostle of Infinity,
And mirror truth's translucent gleam;
He is a dreamer, let him dream.

He is a dreamer; for all time
His mind is married unto rhyme,
Light that ne'er was on land or sea
Hath blushed to him in poetry.
He is a dreamer, and hath caught
Close to his heart a hope, a thought,—
A hope of immortality;
He is a dreamer, let him be.

He is a dreamer; lo! with thee
His soul doth weep in sympathy;
He is a dreamer, and doth long
To glad the world with happy song.
He is a dreamer—in a breath
He dreams of love, and life, and death.
Oh, man! oh, woman! lad and lass,
He is a dreamer, let him pass.

UP TO THE REALM

Up to the realm where she doth reign,
    Unto its utmost holy height,
Through all the muse's dear domain,
    The poet's path is one of light.

But if the way were bleak and long,
    And from the night no friendly spark,
To see her face—O child of song!—
    Who would not leap into the dark?

THE GALAXY

THE Night is soon to wed the Day,
   And for the virgin pale
Hath wrought a multitude of stars
   Into a bridal veil.

BEFORE THE STORM

THE old oak wakes from peaceful sleep,
   Roused by the earth's alarms,
And frightened baby breezes leap
   Into his outstretched arms.

QUATRAIN

THE night is a moonlit garden,
The night is a starry feast,
And the white-rose Sun, at dawning,
Unfolds his petals in the east.

QUATRAIN

GOD made the Night, and, marvelling how
That she might be most ravishingly fair,
He orbed the moon upon her beauteous brow,
And meshed a myriad stars within her hair.

BOHEMIA

BOHEMIA is the land for me;
  Its mountains tower heaven high,
Its singing rivers seek the sea,
  Its cloud-craft sail the ocean sky;
Out of the close embrace of Night,
  Burning with blushes, comes the Dawn;
Bohemia hath the rarer light,—
  The light that leads the poet on.

Bohemia is the land for me;
  There Shakespeare, Milton, Byron, Keats
Plucked from its heart the mystery,
  Walked in its ways and rapt retreats;
It is a land whose splendors smite
  When sun and moon and stars are gone,
It is the land where shines the light,—
  The light that leads the poet on.

Bohemia is the land for me;
    It is the purple land of dreams,
Where one may quaff the nectary
    Of noble thoughts and lofty themes;
Though Sorrow hath a cheek of white
    And Hunger's face be pinched and wan,
Dear God! the more we love the light,—
    The light that leads the poet on.

Bohemia is the land for me;
    It is the rosy realm of rhyme,
Of music, art, and ecstasy,
    It is the clime of deeds sublime;
And o'er it all by day and night,
    And past the portals of the dawn,
The gleaming, beaming, streaming light
    Shall ever lead the poet on.

SERENADE

GOOD-NIGHT, the day has slipped to sleep;
   Good-night, my love, good-night;
The stars are tears the heavens weep;
   Good-night, my love, good-night.
Sweetness and beauty, goodness, grace,
And happiness are in thy face;
Where thou art hallowed is the place;
   Good-night, my love, good-night.

Good-night, once more upon my breast,
   Good-night, my love, good-night;
My heart the haven, stay and rest;
   Good-night, my love, good-night.
Sweetheart, my own, or ere I go,
Once more,—dear love, I love thee so,
Once more—O ecstasy of woe!
   Good-night, my love, good-night.

CHARLOTTE CORDAY

THE canvas speaks; again we see
Marat in death's dark agony;
Again the throng whose weeping eyes
Saw thy pure spirit seek the skies.

The canvas speaks; behind the bars,
Immortal as the steadfast stars,
Thy soul still shines with holy light,
Kindled in Revolution's night.

The canvas speaks; away! away!
In cloisters hooded friars pray
Repose to one who drew the lance
From out the bleeding breast of France.

The canvas weeps; adieu! adieu!
Forever live the brave and true;
Music and marble, brush and rhyme,
Treasure thy memory for all time.

TO LIFT MEN UP

To lift men up, oh, this mine aim,—
Away with pomp and pride and fame,—
Through light and darkness, fire and flame,
　　　To lift men up.

Dear God! for me no crown or state,
No love alone for low or great,
But for one vast humanity,

With hearts as restless as the sea,
And souls serene through suffering;
For them, for these, still let me sing,
　　　To lift men up.

ON THE FLY-LEAF

HERE find we peace and tumult, hope, despair,
Now feel we winter's wind, now Arden's air;
There vice its curse a Caliban doth show
Next maid Miranda, chaste as virgin snow;
This page a scene of cruel carnage brings,
And this, a bridal bed—that couch, a king's;
Cordelia's eye holds pity's melting tear
E'en while the howling tempest echoes Lear.
O mighty soul! who in one fleeting breath
Could picture hell and heaven, life and death,
Base-born the slave who can thy precepts quote
And thank not God a Shakespeare lived and wrote.

A COMFORTER

Vexed with the trials of a dismal day,
I sat me down to rail at God and man,
To pour into a bitter venomed lay
All vile anathema, a curse, a ban ;
Hope seemed to stumble on her weary way,
And a dark purpose like a river ran
Through my sad soul. But how, oh, friend, I pray,
Can one long murmur at the ordained plan,
When to the haven of his arms there slips
A baby daughter robed in snowy white,
Who, with love's prattle on her infant lips,
Has come to kiss and bid me sweet good-night,
And whispers, cuddling close her precious head,
" I'm sleepy, papa ; come, put me to bed" ?

THIS WINTER NIGHT

THIS winter night, against the pane,
I hear the beating of the rain;
The mad wind shrieks a harsh refrain
 This winter night.

Within my room, in warmth and light,
The friendly fire blazes bright,
And—God! out in the bitter cold

How many mortals wander on,
With love and hope and gladness gone,
Poor human sheep outside the fold,
 This winter night!

ROMEO AND JULIET

I.

O Moon, didst thou see, that night, sweet night,
  'Neath thy mellow beams and the stars aglow,
Juliet, with eyes of love and light,
  Close in the arms of Romeo ?

II.

And, Moon, hast thou seen the night, sad night,
  When Verona ran with bated breath,
And wept at the cruel, piteous sight
  Of the ill-starred pair in the arms of death ?

WHEREFORE?

When no sweet thoughts will come to thee
    And harbor in thy heart,
When no dear dreams of ecstasy
    Will woo thy lips apart;

When no rose-rhyme shall bloom for thee
    In gardens God doth give,
Though thine the all of land and sea,
    Wherefore, O poet, live?

THE RAIN

O THE rain, the summer rain,
Kissing all the growing grain,
And the sudden little showers
Giving fragrance to the flowers!
Every streamlet runs along
With a sweeter, clearer song,
To the river, then the main.
O the rain, the rain, the rain!

O the rain, the winter rain,
Beating through the broken pane,
Where with weary heart and brain
Many weep in vain, in vain!
Poor, so poor that hope is dead,
And the children cry for bread.
God, the sorrow! God, the strain!
O the rain, the rain, the rain!

GOOD-BY

WE say at noon and in the night,
  Good-by, good-by, good-by;
Though tears at parting blind the sight,
  Good-by, good-by, good-by.
Over the vasty deep we go
Unto a land afar, and lo!
One little word to tell the woe,
  Good-by, good-by, good-by.

To father, mother, husband, wife,
  Good-by, good-by, good-by;
Love is the guiding star of life,
  Good-by, good-by, good-by.
After the death let come what may,
Our deeds shall live for aye and aye,
And consecrate our peaceful clay,
  Good-by, good-by, good-by,

A LYRIC

A LYRIC, love, for you, my love,
A lyric ; words that weep
And thoughts that pray shall creep
Into my song and kneel to thee.
For you, my love, a lyric.

A lyric, love, for you, my love,
A lyric ; oh, sweetly slain am I ;
One dagger glance from thy dark eye
Hath done the deed—I swoon, I die.
For you, my love, a lyric.

A lyric, love, for you, my love,
A lyric ; all the south
Hath not the honey of thy mouth,
The beauty of thy bosom, love.
For you, my love, a lyric.

A lyric, love, for you, my love,
A lyric; soul of mine,
Never had mortal sweeter shrine
Than where I worship, while I sing
For you, my love, a lyric.

HE IS NOT OLD

HE is not old whose eyes are bright,
Whose bosom throbs, whose heart is light;
Though fourscore be his years enrolled,
If yet he loves, he is not old.
O'er him whose inmost thought is true
The sky of winter beameth blue;
For if a man have heart of gold,
Though white his hair, he is not old.

Age only rests upon the throng
Who live in strife, who cherish wrong;
For oh, 'tis vice that makes us cold,
And then, alas! we soon grow old.
So, friend, and thou wouldst ever be
A man of mirth, not misery,
Be just and gentle, brave and bold,
And then thou never need'st be old.

IN LIGHTER VEIN

In lighter vein, one might indite
To Preciosa something trite,
Liken her eyes to stars of night,
   In lighter vein.

In lighter vein; but softly stay:
When one doth writhe in grievous pain,
With fevered brow and burning brain,

When shadows chase the sun away,
And every infant hope is slain,
How can one write, I pray, I pray,
   In lighter vein?

THE PLAY IS O'ER!

THE play is o'er! my lady wept
The last act through; Othello crept
To Desdemona's feet and died.
O maddened Moor—ill-fated bride,
     The play is o'er!

Homeward we go, while music sweet
Still haunts our ears; across the street
Two shots ring out—the tramp of feet.

Then hastily they bear away
On one rude couch the lifeless clay.
A jealous fool—his mistress gay,
     The play is o'er!

IN OLDEN TIME

In olden time a bonny maid,
A cavalier and his cockade,
A bit of sunshine and of shade
    In olden time.

He wooed the winsome woman till
She yielded to his sovereign will,
And to the farthest gates of death

Love, love was their sweet shibboleth ;
And happiness and joy untold
Blossomed within their hearts of gold
    In olden time.

SOME WORDS

Some words there be of infamy,
  And others dearer than delight;
Some whiter than a June noonday,
  Some blacker than a starless night;

Some—but for me can never be
Lute notes of sweeter ecstasy
Than those fond words of love that drip
Like honey from my lady's lip.

SONNET

DRUNK with delight, the rose I gave her dreams
Upon the billowed bosom of my love ;
It falls and rises with the waves thereof,
And hath forgot the Sun-God's ardent beams ;
A softer summer now doth compass it,
At anchor in the harbor of her heart.
No more for thee, O rose ! the night starlit,
Dawn's magic, or the noontide's golden art,
But rarer rapture shall these joys eclipse
If she absolve thee once with her sweet lips.
Oh, that thy blissful destiny were mine,
   To drink the heavy honey of her breath,
Feel for one day her touch, her clasp divine,
   Sink into sleep and swoon to glorious death !

A DIAMOND

Look how it sparkles, see it greet
    With laughing light the ambient air;
One little drop of sunshine sweet
    Held in eternal bondage there.

CARCASSONNE

The land of love, the land of light,
    The Canaan never cursed with care,
Lies just beyond—so poets write—
    The sunless sea of dark despair.

INTO THE POET'S LIFE

INTO the poet's life one day
A sorrow came in ashen gray,
Into his life a sorrow came
And bowed his head with grief and shame.
It dimmed the lustre of his eye
And stole the sunlight from the sky,
Trampled the tender shoots of truth
And sacked the temple of his youth.

Out of the poet's soul one day
A song of courage sped away,
A song of comfort, hope, and cheer,
Born of a doubt, a sob, a tear,—
Out of his soul, on eagle wing.
O poet rare! thy suffering,
As well as joy, shall light for thee
The ways to immortality.

NOT THOU

God, let me write a rhyme so pure
    That men who read will pray,—
A poem pure that will endure
    Unto the latest day!

This my heart's hope, but on a scroll
    Unfolded to my sight
I read, " Not thou, whose secret soul
    Is damned and black as night!"

WHEN THE MOOD IS ON

When the mood is on, oh, the cunning then,
And the rapture rare of the poet's pen!
The singing soul soars away, away,
And the happy heart hath holiday.
The sky is clear, all the clouds are gone,
When the mood is on, when the mood is on.

When the mood is on, from the earth to sky,
In a frenzy fine rolls the poet's eye;
He hath no sorrow, he hath no care,
A spirit of joy is everywhere;
'Tis a golden day with a diamond dawn,
When the mood is on, when the mood is on.

When the mood is on, to the western Ind
No jewel fair as Rosalind,
And all learn lessons true and good
From the rocks and trees of the Arden wood;
'Tis an age of beauty, brain, and brawn,
When the mood is on, when the mood is on.

But soft, there are faces pinched and drawn
And hearts that bleed when the mood is on;
There are those who weep beside their dead,
There are hungry hosts who cry for bread
Through the long, long night and, alas ! the dawn,
When the mood is on, when the mood is on.

IN SHAKESPEARE LAND

In Shakespeare Land are sylvan scenes,
Hills heaven high and broad demesnes,
Princes, courtiers, kings, and queens
    In Shakespeare Land.

Tybalt is there and Romeo;
" Consort us," quoth Mercutio;
" Have at the villain" so-and-so.

Now, nurse, to gentle Juliet go
And bid her weep and fast and pray;
Woe, woe betide this fatal day
    In Shakespeare Land!

SOLE EMPRESS

A THOUSAND dreams of duty haunt my heart,
  A thousand passions beat about my brain,
An ocean-tide of fragrant fancies start
  And burn my being with exquisite pain.

These and a million more besieging things
  Seek to invade my bosom's citadel,
Where she—my lady—reigns supreme and sings,
  Her smile my heaven and her frown my hell.

THE MUSICIAN

THE earth, the sky, the land and sea
For him make sweetest melody;
He hears the faintest flowing note
That ripples from the linnet's throat.

A STORMY NIGHT

ALL night the waves of darkness roar
And break against a starless shore,
All night—then, weary, spent, and wan,
They die upon the dikes of dawn.

A PRAYER

NOT faith and hope and charity
   Alone secure the soul's success ;
O ye immortal Gods, to me
   Give fearlessness, give fearlessness !

RESOLUTION

O GOD, for strength to turn
   Our souls to ventures vast !
And, pressing on, behind us burn
   The bridges of the past.

THE POET

MOST mighty of magicians he
Who, with some subtle sorcery,
Can kiss a cold, forbidding truth
To beauty and immortal youth.

A DERELICT

AN ocean outcast, baffled, blown
    By every wind and wave;
In death not even poor "Unknown"
    Above his lonely grave.

ADOWN THE YEARS

PERHAPS I may
  Have gone amiss,
To steal one day
  From her a kiss;
But heaven knows
  I'd suffer pain
And direst woes
  To kiss again.

'Twas long ago,
  And yet I vow
It thrilled me so
  It seems as now,
And through the mist
  Of many years
The girl I kissed
  I see in tears.

That she should cry
    And rail at fate
Was more than I
    Dare contemplate;
So on that day,
    Adown the years,
I kissed away
    Her pretty fears.

Sing, poet, sing
    Of that you will,
The sweetest thing
    Is love's first thrill;
And, of all joys,
    The height of bliss
Is but a boy's
    First loving kiss.

LOOKING SEAWARD

I.

THY breasted billows rise and fall,
O breathing sea !
Some joy doth hold thy soul in thrall
Of ecstasy.

II.

And so, my love, my life, my sweet,
Whate'er may be,
Thus should thy billowed bosom beat
At thought of me.

HER SOUL IS PURE

HER soul is pure and sweet and white,
    All good is garnered there;
If I might once peep in and write,
    What poem half so fair?

When next across my path she trips,
    This woman wondrous wise,
I'll kiss a lyric from her lips,
    An epic from her eyes.

SO DARK, SO DEAR

DEATH is so dark to youth,
  So cruel, dank, and drear;
Ambition, love, and truth
  All buried in the bier.

Death is so dear to age,
  So sweet the peace and rest;
Nor summer's heat nor winter's rage,
  Hands folded o'er the breast.

TO MY MOTHER

MANY the weary miles between,
But distance yields to love like thine.
Blest miracle! though all unseen,
Closely thy cheek is pressed to mine.

A SUNSET

THE Sun, departing, kissed the summer Sky,
Then bent an instant o'er her beating breast;
She lifts to him a timid, tear-stained eye,
And lo! her blushes crimson all the west.

FAITH

OceaNs nor mountains do I need
  To thunder wisdom down to me ;
The drop of dew, the living seed,   ˥
  All whisper of Infinity.

INSPIRATION

Joy now hath reached her utmost goal
And sunrise bursts upon the soul
When some immortal thought or plan
Runs riot in the mind of man.

SOMEWHERE, AFAR

SOMEWHERE, afar, dear God, we know
    The mountain-height of glory gleams,
For some fame's fragrant breezes blow
    Across the meadow-land of dreams.

THE QUATRAIN

ONLY four scanty lines are there,
    Yet might a master-mind rehearse
All heaven's hope and hell's despair
    Within one little, trembling verse.

EMANCIPATION

GRANDEUR and truth, infinite grace,
And love shine from his kingly face;
Now doth man's visage pure and fair
Reflect God's imaged glory there.

THE HOME-COMING

THROUGH all the day the witching words
  Elude the poet's art,
Till eve; then wingèd thoughts, like birds,
  Fly homeward to his heart.

MAN

THE vilest creature space doth span
Is weak, despised, dishonored man;
The crown of God's immortal plan,
Noble and lofty, fearless man.

ACTION

I KNOW not how some men can lie
In ease and inactivity,
When Nature's children all uplift
Their voices in a song of thrift.

QUATRAIN

WEAK from its war with giant strife,
   A struggling truth lay down to die;
A poet loved it back to life
   And gave it immortality.

DARKNESS

STUMBLING along the ways through space,
   Led by the wanton wind,
No light illumes his furrowed face,—
   The old man Earth is blind!

THE SANCTUM SANCTORUM

Guard well the temple of the mind,
   Its portals keep with care;
No pilgrim thought impure, unkind,
   Should ever enter there.

HER

Hair like to melted midnight,
   And her eyes,—O God, her eyes!
The lips of language ne'er have loosed
   Words worthy their sweet witchcries.

IF THOU WOULDST READ

If thou wouldst read his verse aright,
Deem it a cry from out the night;
No idle theme is pencilled there,
It is his soul's immortal prayer.

THE POET

Through the sweet summer of his years,
Wherever blossom hopes and fears,
He doth pursue his magic art
And hives the honey in his heart.

IN THE YOSEMITE

THE centuries have builded here,
O'er many a rugged rod
Of peak and cave, a temple where
Nature might worship God.

A THOUGHT

My kingdom for a thought!
One deathless thought, one thought to reach
The utmost bounds of human speech;
My kingdom for a thought!

THE MOB

A SURGING sea of maddened men,
　　Curses and cries, that rise and fall;
The stillness of the grave—and then
　　King Death will hold high carnival.

THE DAWN

UPON his tranquil, joyous face
Sorrow hath left no dark'ning trace,
And yet we know the blessèd light
Followed a struggle in the night.

MARCH

WHITHER doth now this fellow flee
    With outstretched arms at such mad pace?
Can the young rascal thinking be
    To catch a glimpse of April's face?

APRIL

MAIDEN, thy cheeks with tears are wet,
    And ruefully thine eyebrows arch;
Is't as they say, thou thinkest yet
    Of that inconstant madcap March?

SHE IS

GENTLE and tender, sweet and true,
Calm as a summer sky of blue,
And in the depths of her dark eyes
Passion, the tiger, couchant lies.

SPRING

A WHISPER on the heath I hear,
   And blossoms deck the waking wood;
Ah! surely now the virgin year
   Is in her blushing maidenhood.

OVERHEARD

I LINGERED listening 'neath the tree,
    The summer sky above me,
And when a sunbeam kissed a leaf,
    It whispered low, " I love thee."

NIGHT

THE Empress Night hath jewels rare
Of diamond stars within her hair,
And on her beauteous bosom soon
She'll wear the silver crescent moon.

THE END.